Might goes hand in hand with right as He-Man and the Masters of the Universe fight to make their planet safe. The greatest of their enemies is Skeletor, the Lord of Destruction, and his evil band, whose hatred for their foes is never-ending. The war goes on but who will win?

First edition

© LADYBIRD BOOKS LTD MCMLXXXIII and MATTEL INC MCMLXXXIII

MASTERS
OF THE UNIVERSE

A Trap For He-Man

by John Grant
illustrated by Robin Davies

Ladybird Books Loughborough

The twin moons of planet Eternia shone
brightly over the weird peaks of the Mystic
Mountains. On the summit of a mighty crag
stood Skeletor, Lord of Destruction. Below in
the eternal darkness of the Valley of Osgor a
swarm of his slaves -- the Shadow Men -- toiled
to heave a giant crystal of mentalite on to a flat
rock.

The Shadow Men scurried away as their evil
lord stood in their midst and pointed his energy
blade at the crystal. "Now, He-Man," he

exclaimed in triumph, "I shall prepare a trap
for you from which there will be no escape.
Your strength may be that of ten men, but I
have at my command a hundred times ten of
the Shadow People. In the endless night of
Osgor you will be as a blind man, and they will
bear you down to your destruction."

Skeletor's eyes glowed as he prepared to
release his pent-up thought energy.

A blinding bolt shot from Skeletor's energy-blade, making the mentalite blaze with inner power. He aimed his thoughts at the crystal, which took them and set them speeding faster than light across the sleeping planet to Castle Grayskull. There Teela the warrior goddess lay deep in sleep.

As Eternia's red sun rose, Teela woke up. It was barely day-break, but someone was calling her. There was no sound, but clearly in her mind rang the words:

"Teela! It is I, He-Man, who summons you!"

6

He-Man, most powerful of the Masters of the
Universe, only summoned his companions in
arms in times of great peril.

Ordering her servants to make her horse
ready, Teela seized Kobra, the power sceptre
which was both energy weapon and the means
of her power over animals.

Within moments she was galloping across the
jaw-bridge in answer to the summons.

Generating a video-lens with his energy-blade, Skeletor watched as Teela's horse bore her swiftly across the land.

"When she discovers that it was not He-Man but *I* who summoned her, it will be too late . . . and she is the bait to lure that muscle-bound meddler into my trap."

Teela was fast approaching a rocky outcrop when her horse shied, and Kobra glowed with pulsing light as it sensed danger. A vast shape, part lion part reptile, rose above the rocks. Still clutching Kobra, Teela was flung to the ground by her frightened mount. Jumping to her feet, she faced the snarling monster.

The eyes of Kobra glowed red, holding the monster's gaze.

"I know your kind," cried Teela. "You are one of the liozard people. I mean you no harm. Go in peace."

She lowered Kobra and, released from the energy sceptre's magical power, the liozard turned away, and was swiftly lost to view.

Where the land dropped steeply down to the Ocean of Gnarl, Teela reined in her horse. He-Man's message sounded from directly ahead, from the far shore. Would she have to make the long journey around? She scanned the beach. There was no craft of any sort. Holding Kobra aloft she beamed out desperate thought waves: "Help me, He-Man. Which way must I go?"

Then, a speck in the sky caught her attention. The speck grew bigger. It was Stratos, the winged warrior.

"I will bear you on your way,"
cried Stratos. "A summons from
the Lord He-Man to one is a
summons to all."

Teela dismounted and spoke to her horse.
"Return to Castle Grayskull." And as the horse
wheeled and galloped obediently away, she
wrapped her arms around the powerful body of
Stratos and rose with him high into the morning
sky.

From a lone, rocky islet a sharp-eyed sea-dweller spotted the speeding Stratos and his fair passenger. Through the dim caverns of the Sea-world his warning echoed: "Master! Master! ENEMIES!"

From his inner grotto, Mer-Man, ocean war-lord and servant of Skeletor, used aquapower to mind-scan the air and sky above.

"Stratos! Teela!" he hissed. "They will be mine and I will win favour of the Lord Skeletor. Better! I will bargain with my Lord of Destruction for a share of his power in return for my prisoners."

The video-beam of aquapower became a whirling column of water reaching high above the surface of the sea, forming a water spout. Then a second one. And a third. Soon, half a dozen twisting columns of water reached to the clouds and the soaring Stratos.

"Brace yourself!" he cried to Teela. "This is the evil work of Mer-Man!"

Even as he spoke the water spouts found them.

Stratos banked and rolled as the whirling
water spouts twisted about him. His feathers
heavy with sea-water, he was steadily losing
height. Teela's fingers slipped on his wet body.
Then, for a moment Stratos was surrounded by
the spiralling water and Teela was snatched
from him. Down she spun inside the water spout
towards the cold, dim world of the Sea People.

As the waters closed over the warrior goddess,
Mer-Man blasted a stream of zero-energy from

his weapon, imprisoning her in a frozen bubble of crystal-clear ice. Quickly she aimed Kobra at the ice, but the power sceptre was made useless by the zero-energy.

She was weaponless.

"Your toy cannot help you now," laughed Mer-Man. "And *my* people are of the sea and care nothing for your magic sceptre. Here you will stay to await the pleasure of My Lord Skeletor."

Ignoring Mer-Man's mocking words, Teela gripped Kobra and brought all her mind-energy to bear on the distress call of the Masters of the Universe. And slowly the Kobra head began to glow. It grew brighter, as dimly beyond the walls of her ice-bubble prison a dark shape loomed through the green darkness. Kobra flashed rapidly, and Teela felt her mind being probed by strange thought waves.

A giant narwhal swam into view. Its small eyes gleamed, and its ivory tusk caught the faint under-sea light. Teela picked up its thoughts.

"Who has imprisoned you who are of the air?"

"Your master, Mer-Man," replied Teela.

"No master of mine, that creeping sea-slug. I too am of the air. I too have warm blood," replied the narwhal. It backed off a short distance, then with a crash it shattered the ice with its tusk and Teela was borne swiftly upwards on its back.

By a lonely beach on the far shore, Teela bid
farewell to the narwhal. Beyond the beach lay
dense forest filled with the sounds of wild
animals. Teela pushed through the
undergrowth. It would be a long and weary
journey on foot to the other side of the forest.

Kobra began to glow, and at the same
moment something big came crashing through
the trees towards her. It was a giant stag, and it
stood trembling before the bright glow of the
red eyes of Kobra.

"You must carry me on your broad back swiftly to the Lord He-Man," said Teela, as the stag knelt for her to mount. In a moment they were travelling faster than the wind through the forest.

With a piercing shriek a shaggy half-animal figure sprang in front, and the stag skidded to a halt.

"Beast-Man!" cried Teela, holding up Kobra.

Beast-Man flinched and turned his eyes away from the pulsing sceptre, at the same time sending his stun whip lashing out at Teela.

Swerving to avoid the flailing whip, Teela put her heels to the stag. With a roar of rage Beast-Man raised his weapon again, but a charge from Kobra bowled him off his feet as Teela urged her mount to even greater speed.

The savage Beast-Man lumbered in pursuit for a few paces, then seizing a low branch he swung himself into a tree and continued the chase through the tree-tops.

Steadily Teela drew away from her pursuer. But, what was that ahead? Through the trees there was a glint of water; a lake over whose dark surface mists and vapours drifted, and in whose murky depths strange reptiles lurked.

There was no way across. She would have to go around.

Along the lake shore galloped Teela, while fierce eyes watched and clutching claws reached out from the water as she passed.

Round the narrow end of the evil lake sped
the stag and Teela. Not far behind, Beast-Man
raced through the branches, swinging his great
bulk from tree to tree, hand over hand on the
tangle of creepers growing through the leaves.
And there, across a narrow arm of the lake, he
caught a glimpse of his quarry. The forest
reached out far from the bank on both sides.
Clutching a loose strand of vine, Beast-Man
swung up and out over the lake.

Teela glimpsed the flying figure and turned to aim an energy-blast. The stag reared at the blaze of fire and her aim went wide, missing Beast-Man . . . but striking a tree branch just as his clutching fingers closed around it. With a shriek of terror he hurtled headlong into the water.

Instantly the water was aboil as the creatures of the lake swarmed to the attack.

Lashing out with his whip and the broken tree
branch, Beast-Man fought his way to the bank.
Bruised and battered he dragged himself clear
of the water. Trembling with rage, he raised his
great arms above his head and bellowed out his
terrifying battle cry. The animals of the forest
cowered at the awful sound, and the stag
quickened its pace as the sound echoed through
the trees behind.

Bright sunlight showed ahead. They were
almost out of the forest. Once on the open plain
the stag could easily outstrip lumbering Beast-
Man.

Teela raised herself and turned to see how close their pursuer had come. And in that moment the stag lowered its head and ran beneath a low, overhanging tree branch. The branch caught Teela across the shoulders and she was swept from her mount to land, stunned, on the ground while the stag raced on its way in terror at the approach of Beast-Man.

25

Beating his chest in triumph, Beast-Man picked up the unconscious warrior goddess and slung her across his shoulder. Then he set off to seek his lord, Skeletor, and claim a reward for such a valuable prize.

As Beast-Man loped across the dusty plain of Eternia, a speck appeared high in the sky above him. Was it a bird? A cruising wind-raider?

It was Stratos, dried out and desperately seeking Teela. Now, his sharp eyes easily picked up the movement of Beast-Man far below, and he quickly saw that the limp bundle on his shoulder was the warrior goddess. Unaware that he had been spotted, Beast-Man hurried on.

Stratos banked away. There was only one person who could help Teela in her plight. Stratos used every ounce of air-power in his body to reach He-Man before it was too late.

He-Man, in his guise of the weakling Prince Adam, saw Stratos approaching. He raised his sword and cried, "By the power of Grayskull!" changing into He-Man even as he spoke. Quickly Stratos told his story.

"This is the evil work of Skeletor," said He-Man. "Where was Beast-Man headed?"

"The Mystic Mountains," replied Stratos.

"That means only one thing," said He-Man. "The Valley of Osgor. Superpower is useless in that place of eternal night and the fiendish Shadow Men. I will need cunning . . . and my faithful Battle-Cat."

Soon, astride the armoured Battle-Cat, and carrying his battle-axe and shield, He-Man was travelling swiftly across the rolling plains of Eternia towards the ragged peaks of the planet's high mountains and the smothering darkness of the Valley of Osgor.

The sun was high in the sky when He-Man looked into the blackness of the grim chasm where Teela was held captive.

29

In the deepest part of the Valley of Osgor,
Skeletor stood before his prisoner, who was held
helpless against a stone pillar by bands of pure
energy. "Welcome to the Dark Valley, Teela,
Warrior Goddess," he sneered. "Very soon you
may join me in welcoming our dear friend He-
Man. It is too bad for him that he is all that
stands between me and supreme power in the
Universe."

"Do not be so sure, Skeletor," cried Teela,
defiantly.

"But I *am* sure," replied Skeletor. "His may be the mightiest body in the Universe, but mine is the mightiest brain. I have conceived a trap in which you are the bait. My slaves the Shadow People are the jaws which will snap shut and crush him once and for all."

A Shadow-Man slithered out of the gloom and crouched low before Skeletor.

"My lord, the lookouts report the approach of your enemy."

He-Man paused on the rim of the gorge. A winding track led down below the over-hanging cliffs which had kept out the light of day since the beginning of time. Once into that deadly shade he was at the mercy of the Shadow-Men. Their great strength was their ability to see in the dark. But so, like all of his tribe, could Battle-Cat. Light meant agony to the Shadow-Men. And this was their great weakness. It was with light that He-Man would defeat them.

The sun had reached its highest point when He-Man unslung his Battle-Shield. Holding it out, he caught the rays of the sun and sent them reflecting on to the rocks. Mounting Battle-Cat, he urged the great beast down the narrow track, all the time holding the glittering metal shield to catch the sun, and sending a dazzling beam ahead of him into the murk of the deadly Valley.

He-Man's war mount picked its way quietly among the boulders strewing the path. But to the super-sensitive ears of the Shadow-Men, the silent steps of the huge cat were adequate warning. At a gesture from Skeletor they took up their positions. Gripping crude clubs they ranged about the stone pillar. Others lined the bottom of the gorge on either side, while the remainder perched high up in dark ledges and crevices, ready to leap down upon their intended victim.

Skeletor cast a glance around the final placing of his slaves. All seemed in readiness. Like stars in a black sky the eyes of the Shadow-Men gleamed in the darkness.

The sounds of the approaching victim drew closer. Skeletor looked again. Two larger, brighter stars shone out. A low rumbling growl came from their direction. Then, a great blaze of agonizing brightness leapt at the Shadow-Men, and He-Man was upon them.

In the terrifying brightness of the sunlight reflected from He-Man's shield, the Shadow-Men tumbled screaming from their hiding places among the rocks. Fighting each other in their desperation, they bore down upon Skeletor where he stood beside the captive Teela and the glowing mentalite crystal.

"Back, you cowardly reptiles," screamed the Lord of Destruction. "Perhaps this will help to put some fighting spirit into your miserable hearts!" And, raising his energy blade, Skeletor sent bolt after bolt of crackling power darting among them.

But now, added to the pain of the dazzling light, came the screams of Battle-Cat. Mighty paws slashing right and left, the great cat bounded to the attack.

"Hold on, Teela!" cried He-Man, as the Shadow-Men parted before him, leaving the prisoner unguarded. "And you, Skeletor! Prepare to meet your fate!"

Skeletor again raised his energy blade, but the scrambling Shadow-Men jostled about him in panic, spoiling his aim. He stumbled and was instantly borne to the ground. He struggled to his feet in time to see the precious crystal of mentalite about to be swept from its flat rock, and with a supreme effort he caught it as it fell.

Teela and He-Man watched as the blinded Shadow-Men blundered into their evil lord who held the crystal above his head, out of reach of the struggling mob. Then, suddenly it was knocked flying from his grasp to smash against the black rocks.

In an instant the pent-up energy in the crystal was released, sending a massive shock wave to the very roots of the Valley of Osgor. The overhanging cliffs split from top to bottom and the sunlight blazed down. The rock pillar dissolved into fragments, setting Teela free. As the dust settled, the last Shadow-Man had vanished.

Mounted on Battle-Cat, He-Man and Teela prepared to leave the ruins of the Valley, but, as the last of the dust cloud disappeared there was revealed a dark figure standing amid the shattered rocks.

Skeletor raised his energy blade.

"Once again your meddling has cost me dear," he cried. "But no one escapes unharmed from an encounter with the Lord of Destruction."

A bolt darted from Skeletor's weapon, but, swift as it was, He-Man was swifter. He leapt to the ground, battle-axe swinging ready, and the energy blast passed harmlessly over his head.

A second shot was deflected by the shield, and
He-Man rushed to the attack. Bolt after bolt
crackled harmlessly on the shield while Skeletor
backed into a crevice in the rock before the
gleaming axe.

Once again Skeletor fired. Once more the
powerful battle-shield caught the force of the
bolt, but this time deflected it to strike the rock
face above the crevice. With a rumbling crash
the rocks collapsed, covering and concealing the
crevice and Skeletor.

As He-Man and Teela rode out of the Valley
of Osgor, the rays of the sun were penetrating
into nooks and crannies which had never until
now known its warmth. The poisonous mosses
and lichens which draped the black rocks
shrivelled and died.

Teela pointed to a spot high above them. The
collapsing rocks had released a spring of clear
water, and now it cascaded in a glittering
stream to form the beginnings of a river on the
valley floor.

"Sun and water," said Teela. "They will bring the grass and trees and flowers. Soon, Osgor will be as fair a spot as any place on planet Eternia."

"Yes," replied He-Man. "When evil is defeated, good can flourish for the benefit of all."